Bella
dancerella™

Concert Night

3

Written by
Poppy Rose

ABC
Books

Illustrated by
Omar Aranda

Miss Tweedle's Ballet School concert was coming up soon and Bella was at the Pretty Plié store being fitted for her costumes. 'Look at that tiara on the shelf, Dad!' Bella exclaimed. 'It's so sparkly and pretty.'

'Very pretty,' Dad replied. 'But there are tiaras and headdresses in the attic at home.'

'What if they're not the same as the ones the other girls are wearing on concert night?' Bella asked as she popped the tiara on her head.

'They'll be fine,' said Dad, glancing at the tiara's price tag. 'Buying *three* costumes for the *Swan Lake* performance is expensive enough. We can't afford headdresses as well.'

Bella bit her bottom lip and gently placed the tiara back on its cushion. 'I know,' she said, dreamy eyes still fixed on the gorgeous headdress. 'I love being a swan with all the other girls. I don't understand why I have to be Charlotte's understudy for the role of Princess Odette. There's no way she's going to miss being the star of the concert!'

'I know I won't have to take Charlotte's place,' Bella continued, 'but Miss Tweedle said I have to be prepared just in case. So we have to buy my swan costume as well as the two Princess Odette ones.'

'Oh goodness, no!' cried Miss Penny, the storeowner, as she came in from the other room carrying two magnificent costumes with layers and layers of beaded tulle. 'You don't buy the lead-role costumes,' she said to Bella and her dad. 'You hire them!'

Bella rushed towards the costumes Miss Penny was holding. 'Look at the jewels on them,' she whispered in awe. 'They're the *prettiest* costumes ever! They're Charlotte's for the lead role, aren't they?'

Miss Penny shook her head. 'Charlotte's costumes are the same as these and hanging out the back. She's already had her fitting. These are yours to use if you have to take Charlotte's place. Let's pop the white one on so I can adjust it to fit you perfectly. I can adjust the other one then without you having to try it on.'

'They're mine?!' Bella gasped. 'Do I get to take them home?'

'Well, no, not today,' answered Miss Penny. 'After the fitting the costumes stay here until a week before the performance. You can pick them up the Saturday before the concert.'

'Oh,' Bella said, her smile fading. 'That's ages away.'

'Let's try this on, shall we?' Miss Penny suggested brightly.

Bella watched as Miss Penny walked towards the change rooms with the costume. 'I can't wait to try it on!' Bella called to her. *And I know the perfect thing to go with it,* she thought. Bella plucked the tiara from its cushion then raced past Dad into the change rooms.

When Bella walked out towards the mirrors dressed
as Princess Odette, Dad caught his breath. 'Look at
you, my beautiful Bella!' he said with a sigh.

'I'm a princess!' Bella cried, *twirling* and whirling,
snatching glimpses of her reflection as she did.
'Please can we get the tiara as well, Dad? Please?'

11

Dad shook his head and slowly removed the tiara.
'No, Bella, we're just getting costumes, remember,'
he answered quietly. 'Why don't you get changed
while we settle everything here?'

Bella took one last look at herself in the mirror.
'I'll see you in two more weeks, Princess Odette,'
she said to her reflection with a giggle.

When Bella stepped out of the change room, Miss Penny handed her a big white box with a green bow. 'Here's your swan costume, Bella,' she said.

'Thank you!' Bella said, taking the box.

That afternoon, out in the barn, Bella was struggling with her Princess Odette routines.

'She missed another step!' quacked Puddles as he flapped his wings in alarm.

'Oops!' honked Waddles as he covered his eyes with his wings.

'Oh dear, she's really messing it up now,' neighed Jasper as he swished the beat out even louder with his tail.

'STOP!' bleated Chloe as she threw her hooves up in frustration.

15

'I give up,' Bella sobbed, dropping to the barn floor.
'I can do my swan routines perfectly, but this Princess
Odette role is just too hard. What does it matter
anyway? We all know I won't be dancing it on the night.'

'Hush, hush,' clucked Agatha, wiping away Bella's tears. 'Some things take a lot of practice to get right. Isn't that so, little chicks?' The chicks snuggled in around Bella and nodded their heads in agreement.

'But what if I never get it right, Aggie?' Bella asked.

'If only you had your Princess Odette costume already,' woofed Roy, laying his head in Bella's lap. 'You do the dance of the swans perfectly when you wear your swan costume. Maybe being dressed for the part helps you to remember your steps.'

'Roy's right,' squeaked Maggie, jumping into Bella's palm.

'That's it!' bleated Chloe, barging in on the tight little group. 'The chest in the attic! There's bound to be something amongst your mother's things that might help. Let's go and look.'

Up in the attic, everyone gathered eagerly round the chest.

'My mum's ballet chest,' whispered Bella. 'Dad said it was filled with special things that were just for me.'

Out came feathers and tutus, wands and wraps.

Next came pointe shoes and slippers and **black shoes** with **taps.**

Then came the costumes: **blues**, **pinks** and whites .

Last came the headdresses and Bella's squeals of **delight!**

'Try this on,' woofed Roy as he nudged a box with a tiara towards Bella.

Bella lifted the tiara from its cushion and gasped. 'Roy!' she cried. 'This is even prettier than the one in the Pretty Plié store that I wanted.'

Bella stood before the mirror and sat the tiara in place. As she did she felt a funny tingle rush from her head and travel down the back of her neck.

'**I'm Princess Odette,**' she gasped, staring at the reflection in the mirror. 'How can that be?'

The animals held their breath as Bella began to dance the Princess Odette routines. And as she danced the only sound to be heard was the gentle sweep of Bella's shoes on the attic's timber floorboards.

'Extraordinary,' bleated Chloe as Bella completed the routines. 'Not a step wrong.'

'Her technique was flawless,' neighed Jasper from the doorway.

'And her timing was perfect,' squeaked Maggie. 'Without music to help her.'

'Magnificent,' quacked Puddles. 'Exquisite,' honked Waddles. 'You did it,' woofed Roy. 'You did it!'

Bella was amazed. 'I did do it, didn't I? I can't believe it.'

She glided over to the mirror and took another look.
It's only me who sees this reflection in the Princess Odette costume, she thought. *Am I imagining it?*

Bella stared at the mirror and removed her tiara.
It's just me, she thought. Then she put the tiara back on.
And now I'm Odette! Bella took the tiara off and then
put it back on again and again.

'What are you doing, Bella?' Agatha asked with a frown.
'Are you okay?'

'Oh... Um... Sure, Aggie,' Bella answered, clutching
the tiara to her chest.

For the next three weeks Bella practised her routines.

She danced as a princess and she danced as a swan.

When she danced without the tiara, she got
her Odette steps wrong.

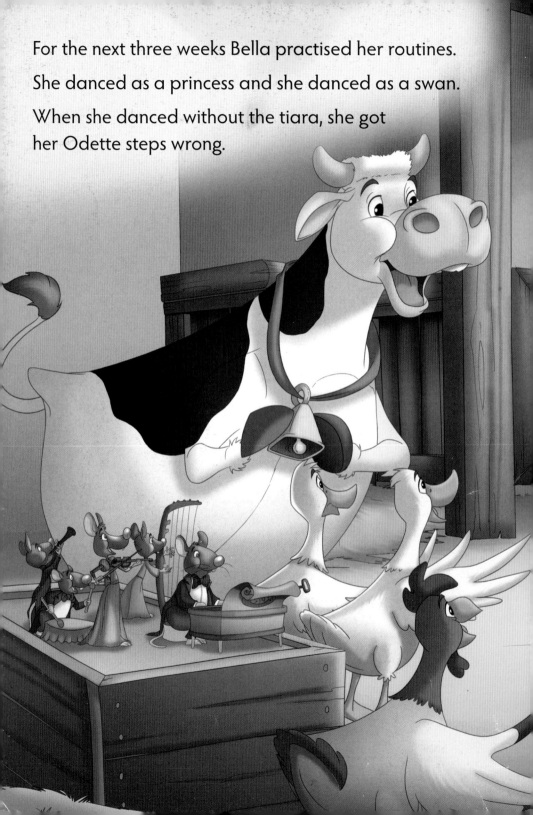

When the day of the concert finally arrived, Bella could dance the Princess Odette role perfectly, but only when she wore her mum's tiara.

'I'll see you when rehearsals are over,' Dad said to Bella. 'We'll have just enough time to get something to eat, then you have to be back here for tonight.'

'I'm soooooo excited!' Bella said as she gave Roy a hug and then waved goodbye.

Excerpts from
Swan Lake

performed by
Miss Tweedle's
Ballet School

The theatre's dressing room was a flurry of excited activity.

'We'll start with the dance of Princess Odette as the Swan Queen,' Miss Tweedle announced. 'Then we'll do the dance of the swans. **Bella**, *you can dance alongside Charlotte as her understudy.*'

Bella quickly changed into her blue Swan Queen costume and placed her tiara on her head.

'Where did you get that tiara?' Charlotte snapped. 'It's way too pretty for you to wear. You're just the silly understudy. I think we should swap.'

'It belonged to my mum and I'm not allowed to lend it to anybody, sorry,' Bella answered.

Charlotte and Bella stepped onto the stage and the music began. The two girls danced in perfect time. When they'd finished, Miss Tweedle clapped and said, *'Absolutely beautiful!* Now quickly change for the dance of the swans, Bella, and you can have a break, Charlotte.'

Back in the dressing room, Charlotte watched Bella put her tiara into her bag. She helped Bella change into her swan costume and then ushered her and the other swans out. Now Charlotte was alone.

'Now that I've gotten rid of her it's time to try on that super-pretty tiara,' Charlotte whispered, and she took the tiara from Bella's bag.

Charlotte popped the tiara on her head and danced from mirror to mirror looking at herself. 'It looks so much better on me,' she said to the first mirror as she spun past.

'I'm the real Princess Odette after all!' she called to the second mirror as she *leapt* and *twirled*.

Charlotte was so busy looking at herself that she
didn't see the stool in front of the third mirror.
She crashed into the stool and flew right over it.

Charlotte landed with a crunch on top of the tiara.
'OOOOH!' she cried. 'My ankle!'

Charlotte sat up and looked at the tiara.
It was in pieces. **'Oh no!'** she wailed in a panic.
'It belonged to Bella's mum. What am I going to do?'
She bent down and quickly scooped up the pieces.
Then she hopped over to her ballet bag and hid
them right down the bottom under everything else.

Later that evening, Bella was back at the theatre for concert night. 'You must be especially excited now that you're dancing the lead role,' said Dad as he walked her to the dressing room. 'Poor Charlotte! Miss Tweedle said that she couldn't even stand on her ankle.'

But Bella was too busy rummaging through her ballet bag to respond. 'It has to be here!' she cried. '*Please be here.* **Please!**'

'What have you lost?' asked Dad.

'Mum's tiara,' Bella answered, choking back a sob. 'I can't dance as Princess Odette without it! I have to find it!'

'You must have left it in the dressing room,' Dad said calmly. 'Your bag has been with us since you left rehearsals this afternoon and you haven't opened it once. So it has to be in the dressing room.'

'I know I put it in my bag,' Bella said, feeling her heart race. 'And now it's not there. I won't go on stage without it. I can't and I won't!'

'Calm down and go and get ready,' Dad soothed. 'The tiara will be inside and you will be wonderful tonight. I'll see you on stage.'

Dad gave Bella a kiss and guided her gently through the dressing-room door.

Once inside, Bella rushed over to where she'd gotten changed earlier that day. 'It's not here,' she stammered, sweat trickling down her neck.

'**What are you looking for?**' Melody asked.

'My tiara,' Bella answered. 'I can't dance without it. I just can't!'

'What about this one?' offered Annabelle. 'It's Charlotte's. She left it behind.'

'I need mine,' Bella cried, flopping down on the stool that
Charlotte fell over earlier that day. 'I can't dance as Princess
Odette without it. I get all the steps wrong when I'm not
wearing my mum's tiara. I'll look so stupid. I can't go on.'

'This sounds like a case of stage fright to me, Bella,' Miss
Tweedle said sweetly as she walked into the dressing room.

'Everyone gets it from time to time, but you *will* dance Odette and you'll dance her as beautifully as you did this afternoon. I'm sorry you've misplaced your mother's tiara. It's bound to turn up, but tonight you'll have to wear Charlotte's. Now, take some deep breaths and get dressed. Hurry up. Everyone else is ready.'

When it was time for Bella to go on, she was frozen to the spot on the side of the stage. Then she felt a paw on her back. It was Roy pushing her firmly forwards.

Bella stumbled on stage trembling from head to toe with her eyes shut tight. *I think I'm going to be sick,* she thought as she danced her first shaky steps.

I can't do it. I'm just not good enough.
Then, eyes still closed, Bella suddenly saw a vision of her mother. She was dancing as Princess Odette on stage just like Bella. *I'm dancing with you,* Bella thought with a small smile and she danced the entire routine without a single mistake.

By the time the flock of swans joined her on stage, Bella was feeling much better. She opened her eyes and blinked, but the vision of her mother was gone. *I can still do this*, she thought, counting the steps out in her head and dancing with ease. *I really think I can!*

When it came time for the final Princess Odette
solo, Bella glided back onto centre stage relaxed
and smiling. She looked out at the audience and
spotted Dad and Roy. Bella blew them a quick **kiss**
and danced the solo magnificently.

Bella finished with a deep curtsey to the loudest applause she'd ever heard in her life. She saw her dad standing and cheering and gave him a wave.

Eyes bright with tears and brimming with joy, she curtseyed once more.

'Thanks, Mum,' she said to herself. 'I *did* do it after all!'